SHERLOCK

A Police Dog Story

by Meish Goldish

illustrated by Thomas Andrae

New York, New York

Credits
Cover photo, © Eric Isselée/Shutterstock.

Publisher: Kenn Goin
Senior Editor: Joyce Tavolacci
Creative Director: Spencer Brinker

Library of Congress Cataloging-in-Publication Data

Names: Goldish, Meish, author. I Andrae, Tom, illustrator.
Title: Sherlock : a police dog story / by Meish Goldish ; illustrated by Thomas
  Andrae.
Description: New York, New York : Bearport Publishing, 2017. I Series: Hound
  Town chronicles I Summary: Sherlock the police dog goes after a thief in
  the parking lot of the Hound Town Mall.
Identifiers: LCCN 2016042379 (print) I LCCN 2016043093 (ebook) I ISBN
  9781627248709 (library) I ISBN 9781684020713 (ebook)
Subjects: I CYAC: Mystery and detective stories. I Police dogs—Fiction. I
  Dogs—Fiction.
Classification: LCC PZ7.G56777 Sh 2017 (print) I LCC PZ7.G56777 (ebook) I DDC
  [Fic]—dc23
LC record available at https://lccn.loc.gov/2016042379

For more information, write to Bearport Publishing Company, Inc., 45 West 21st
Street, Suite 3B, New York, New York 10010. Printed in the United States of America.

10 9 8 7 6 5 4 3 2 1

CONTENTS

WELCOME TO HOUND TOWN

A Doggone Nice Place to Live!

Population:
25,000 people
20,000 dogs

CHAPTER 1

"Good Job, Sherlock!"

"Get him!" the police officer shouted.

Sherlock the police dog raced up a ladder, jumped over a brick wall, and then landed on the grass below. In the distance, a man was running. The large German Shepherd charged after him at full speed. Then the dog leaped and knocked the man down. Barking loudly, the **canine** stood over him so he couldn't escape.

The police officer ran over and petted the dog. "Good job, Sherlock!" she cried out and gave Sherlock a treat.

Ten-year-old Jason Park had watched the training exercise in amazement. It was a sunny Saturday morning at the Hound Town Police Academy, where Jason was visiting his aunt Meg, a police officer, her canine partner, Sherlock, and Stuart the dog trainer.

"That's awesome! I can't believe how Sherlock jumped over the wall!" Jason said, turning to his aunt and Stuart.

"He's one of the most talented members of our police **force**," said Aunt Meg.

"Does Sherlock do this every day?" Jason asked.

"Sherlock has to train regularly, just like an athlete. And, every week, we practice different skills," Aunt Meg said. Then she checked the time on her cell phone. "Well, Sherlock and I have to go to work now," she said. She leaned over and gave Jason a hug. Jason rubbed Sherlock's head. Then he hopped on his bike and pedaled home, enjoying the late morning sun on his face.

Jason arrived home just as his father was making lunch. The smell of baked macaroni and cheese **wafted** through the house.

"The macaroni will be ready in a minute," Mr. Park said.

At the kitchen table, Jason dug his fork into the cheesy noodles as he told his family all that Sherlock had done at the Academy.

"You should see how high and far he can leap," he cried. "Sherlock climbed a ladder and flew right over a wall!"

Jason's eight-year-old sister, Katie, smiled. "Too bad Hot Dog can't do that," she joked.

Hot Dog was the family's pet **dachshund**. Her favorite thing to do was curl up in her plushy dog bed.

"Maybe Hot Dog could do those things . . . with the right training," Jason declared.

"Come on, you two," Dad said. "Hot Dog is much too small to climb a ladder."

Jason looked at his mother, a **veterinarian**. "Mom, what do you think?"

"Well," she said smiling. "Who knows? Anything is *paw*-sible."

Mom had a habit of making corny animal jokes.

After lunch, Jason led Hot Dog to the living room. He placed a small stepladder in front of her.

"Climb the steps!" Jason **commanded**.

Hot Dog stood still, staring at the ladder.

"I told you, Einstein," Katie teased. "There's no way a dachshund can climb a ladder. Hot Dog's legs are too short."

Jason lifted Hot Dog and placed her front right leg on the first step of the ladder.

"Now climb, girl," Jason said.

Again, the dog stayed perfectly still. Then she began to lick her paw.

"I said *climb*, not *lick*!"

Jason could hear his parents giggling in the kitchen.

Jason plopped down on the couch and clicked on the television. He was watching a nature show about wolves when the words *Breaking News* flashed across the screen.

"There's been a robbery at the Hound Town Mall. Police investigators are on the scene. More details to follow as the story unfolds," said the reporter.

As Jason watched the screen, he saw Aunt Meg being interviewed at the mall. Jason ran into the kitchen, where his parents were washing the dishes.

"Mom, Dad, there's been a robbery at the mall. I just saw Aunt Meg on TV. Can I ride my bike there to see what's going on?"

His parents looked at each other with concerned expressions.

"Please? I'll be careful," Jason pleaded. "It's only a five-minute ride."

Dad said, "You can go if you promise to stay a safe distance from the police."

"And don't **interfere** with their **investigation**," Mom added.

"I promise I won't. See you later," Jason said as he grabbed his bike helmet and rushed out the door.

With that, Jason was soon pedaling his bike as fast as he could down Mutt Avenue toward the mall.

CHAPTER 2

A Sneaky Thief

Jason rode his bike into the large parking lot of the Hound Town Mall. There were two shiny police cars parked outside The Cat's Meow Jewelry store. He saw Aunt Meg and Sherlock standing near the store and waved.

Aunt Meg walked over to greet Jason. "Hi, Jason," Aunt Meg said. "What brings you here?"

"I heard about the robbery on TV. What happened?" asked Jason.

"Well, someone stole several expensive men's watches from the jewelry store," she said.

Jason's eyes grew wide. "Really?" he asked. "Did anyone see the thief?"

"No," Aunt Meg explained. "Whoever it was managed to take the watches from the display case without being noticed."

"Wow, that's sneaky," Jason exclaimed. "But how could nobody notice?"

"We're trying to figure that out," Aunt Meg said. "The theft occurred about half an hour after the store opened. There were a handful of customers in the store at the time, and a guard was standing at the front door."

"That is weird," Jason said.

"Yes," replied Aunt Meg. "Solving the mystery will take some careful police work."

"I've got to get back to the store, Jason. I need to question the **clerks**."

Jason petted the police dog. "Bye, Sherlock," he said. "Good luck solving the case!" Aunt Meg led Sherlock back into the jewelry store.

I wish I could help Aunt Meg solve this mystery, Jason thought. *But what can I do?*

Jason walked through the parking lot. He wanted to get closer to the jewelry store so he could see exactly what the police were doing. Jason **peered** through the large glass window at the front of the store. Two officers were inside, dusting the display case for fingerprints.

Maybe I can help Aunt Meg and Sherlock by searching for clues, he thought. Then Jason remembered his promise to his parents. He couldn't interfere with the police investigation. So how could he look for clues?

CHAPTER 3

Hunting for Clues

Jason decided to walk around the Hound Town Mall. The Cat's Meow Jewelry store was closed to customers during the police investigation. However, Jason found two stores on either side of the jewelry store that were still open for business.

First he walked into Let's Talk, a cell phone store.

"May I help you?" a clerk asked.

"Oh, uh . . . I'm just **browsing**," Jason replied, as he clumsily picked up and pretended to examine a shiny blue cell phone case.

Then he slowly walked around the store, trying not to draw any more attention to himself. He paused to look at a cell phone with a big screen. As he walked toward the back of the store, he noticed a closed door near the far wall marked, "Exit." Jason thought, *I wonder where that door leads.*

"Excuse me," Jason said to the clerk. "Can I use this door to get to the restroom?" Jason knew the restrooms were actually in the food court, but maybe the clerk would tell him where the door went.

"No, I'm sorry," said the clerk. "That door connects to the jewelry store next door. You can find a restroom in the food court."

"Okay," said Jason. "Thanks for your help!" Then he walked out of the store hiding a small grin on his face.

Jason then entered the shop on the other side of the jewelry store. It was a fancy men's clothing store called Dapper Dan's.

A well-dressed man stood behind a shiny wood counter near the rear of the store. He had on an orange tie covered in polka dots. "Can I help you look for something?" he asked in a friendly voice.

"I'm looking for a special gift for my dad. I think he might like a tie. Where can I find one like yours?" Jason asked.

The clerk led Jason to a large wooden table. On it was an assortment of neatly folded ties arranged by color. "We have a rainbow of colors," said the man.

"You sure do, thanks!" said Jason.

"My pleasure," said the man. "Let me know if you need anything else."

Just then a customer walked into the store. The clerk left Jason's side to greet the shopper.

As Jason studied the ties, he secretly scanned the room. He noticed that this store also had a side door that seemed to exit directly into The Cat's Meow.

Soon, Jason found something else interesting in the clothing shop. In one corner near the side door was a dressing room.

Jason looked at the swinging doors of the dressing room. Something was snagged on the door **hinge**. He took a closer look and found a torn piece of cloth. It was light blue with lace trim.

As Jason **examined** the cloth, it reminded him of something his mother would wear. Then he heard someone walk up behind him. Jason glanced up and saw Aunt Meg and Sherlock standing next to him.

"Aunt Meg," Jason said, "I'm glad you're here. I just found something you might want to see. Take a look at this. It was caught on the hinge of the dressing room door."

"It appears to be fabric from a dress or a woman's scarf," she said. "That's odd. Why would a piece of a woman's scarf get caught on the door hinge of a men's dressing room? A woman wouldn't be trying on clothes in here."

Jason thought for a second. "Maybe the jewelry thief is a woman," he suggested. "Maybe she made her getaway through this store."

Aunt Meg shook her head. "I doubt that," she said. "The jewelry store clerks told me there were no female customers in the store all morning, only males." Aunt Meg paused to think some more.

"Still, it's odd that this fabric would be on the door hinge," she said. "Let's see if Sherlock can help."

CHAPTER 4

High-Speed Chase

Aunt Meg held the fabric up to Sherlock's nose. "Track!" she commanded. The dog sniffed the fabric. Then she said, "Go, Sherlock!"

Suddenly, Sherlock barked. He raced out of the store's entrance and ran into the mall. Aunt Meg quickly followed. Jason darted after them but made sure to keep a safe distance.

Sherlock dashed through the mall. He rounded a corner and ran into a shoe store. He quickly sniffed around the store, pausing at a men's shoe display. Then he spun around, zipping out of the shoe store and past a bookstore. Then he ran to one of the mall's main exits. He barked at the door, which Aunt Meg quickly opened. Then the dog bolted into the parking lot.

Aunt Meg and another police officer followed Sherlock through the parking lot. The dog wove in and out of a maze of parked cars.

Jason continued to follow **steadily** behind so he could see what was going on. He saw Sherlock heading for the far end of the lot. In the distance, he could see a woman pushing a shopping cart filled with several large shopping bags. She was moving toward a parked car.

Suddenly, Sherlock took off at full speed toward the woman as if he was in a race. That's when she spotted the dog running toward her. She spun around and pushed the shopping cart directly at Sherlock. The cart came speeding toward the police dog. *Whoosh!* Sherlock leaped right over it.

Jason couldn't believe his eyes. It reminded him of the practice exercise he had watched earlier that day—only this was real!

The woman then ran to her car and tried to yank open the driver's side door. Sherlock made one final leap and knocked the woman down to the ground.

When Aunt Meg and the other police officer reached the car, Sherlock was standing over the woman barking. That's when they noticed something on the ground lying next to her. It was a wig. The person was a man!

"Sit!" Aunt Meg commanded. Sherlock **obeyed** and sat down next to the fallen man.

Aunt Meg ordered the man to turn over, put his hands behind his back, and stay on the ground.

The other officer searched the shopping bags. He found the stolen watches as well as other stolen goods from the mall!

Aunt Meg handcuffed the **suspect** and placed him into a police car.

"Well, Jason, it looks like we caught our thief," she said smiling.

"That's awesome," Jason said. Then he got a confused look on his face. "But how did Sherlock know that this person was the thief?"

"He didn't know," Aunt Meg explained. "But Sherlock was able to match the scent on the torn fabric with the scent of the thief."

Aunt Meg continued, "After stealing the watches, the thief entered the men's clothing store through the side door. Then he slipped into the changing room to disguise himself as a woman."

"So no one would recognize him as the man who was in the jewelry store?" Jason asked.

"Exactly!" Aunt Meg said. "After stealing the watches, he went on to rob several other stores dressed as a woman. We found lots of other stolen goods."

Jason smiled. "You and Sherlock are both amazing **detectives**!" he exclaimed.

"And you helped us by looking for clues and finding the fabric," Aunt Meg replied. "Great work!"

CHAPTER 5

Try, Try Again

Jason rode his bike home. He couldn't wait to tell his family about his adventure at the Hound Town Mall.

He described everything he had seen and how he had searched for clues.

"And I helped solve the case!" Jason said proudly. "I found a piece of fabric from the thief's clothing!"

"Good work, son!" his father said. "Sounds like you have the makings of a great detective."

Jason thought for a moment. "But I'd need a good police dog to help me," he said.

"Well, don't count on Hot Dog," Katie teased.

Jason gave his sister a serious look. "Why can't I count on Hot Dog?" he asked. "I still think that, with the right training, she'd make a great police dog."

"Okay, then I'd love to see her leap over something the way Sherlock did," Katie said.

"Just you wait," Jason replied.

The next morning, Jason opened the newspaper. The front page had an article about the robbery at the Hound Town Mall. Sherlock's picture was at the top of the page. The caption read: *Sherlock the Police Dog 'Nose' How to Sniff Out a Thief!"*

Hot Dog was stretched out on the living room floor. Jason showed her the newspaper.

"See, Hot Dog," Jason said. "You could be famous, too."

Jason found a toy truck in his room. He took it to the living room and placed it in front of the little dog.

"Okay, girl, let's see you leap over that truck," he said. "Jump!"

Hot Dog stared at the truck but didn't move an inch.

"C'mon, girl! You can do it!" Jason **encouraged** her.

Then he had an idea. "I'll be the thief, Hot Dog. You chase me!"

Hot Dog just stared at Jason.

Mom, Dad, and Katie were watching.

"Mom, how can I get Hot Dog to jump over this truck?" he asked.

"Try putting a bowl of dog food on the other side of it," Mom suggested. "See if she'll leap for her food."

Jason got some food and placed it on the floor, past the truck. Hot Dog walked around the toy truck and began to gobble down the food.

Mom, Dad, and Katie clapped their hands.

"Well," Jason sighed, petting the dachshund. "It's a start."

Sherlock
A Police Dog Story

1. List five words that best describe Jason. Give examples of things he does or says in the story that helped you choose those words.

2. How does Jason help Aunt Meg solve the mystery?

3. Aunt Meg never explains how the thief managed to steal the watches without being noticed. How do you think he may have done it?

4. What makes Sherlock a great police dog? Use examples from the story to support your answer.

GLOSSARY

browsing (BROW-zing) looking at store items, but not for anything in particular

canine (KAY-nine) a dog

clerks (KLURKS) salespeople in a store

commanded (kuh-MAN-did) ordered a person or animal to do something

dachshund (DAHKS-hunt) a type of dog with a long body and short legs

detectives (di-TEK-tivs) people who work to solve crimes

encouraged (en-KUR-ijd) praised a person or an animal to give them confidence

examined (eg-ZAM-uhnd) looked at carefully

force (FORSS) a team of people who work together

hinge (HINJ) a jointed piece on which a door swings

interfere (in-tur-FIHR) to get in the way of

investigation (in-*ves*-tuh-GAY-shuhn) the job of finding out a lot of information about something, such as a crime

obeyed (oh-BAYD) followed instructions

peered (PEERD) looked hard at something that is difficult to see

steadily (STED-ih-lee) in a firm manner

suspect (SUHSS-pekt) someone thought to be responsible for a crime

veterinarian (*vet*-ur-uh-NERR-ee-uhn) a doctor who treats sick or injured animals

wafted (WAFT-id) carried through the air

About the Author

Meish Goldish is an award-winning author of more than 300 books for children. His book *City Firefighters* won a Teachers' Choice Award in 2015. He especially enjoys writing fiction, nonfiction, and poetry about animals. Growing up in Tulsa, Oklahoma, Meish liked to play with the many dogs in his neighborhood. Now a resident of Brooklyn, New York, he continues to frolic among the friendly canines there.

About the Illustrator

Thomas Andrae studied illustration in Hamburg, Germany, and has worked mainly creating storyboards and layouts. Whenever he gets the chance, he also enjoys illustrating comics and children's books. Thomas lives and works near Hamburg and shares his studio and house with two cats and a stray dog he rescued from Spain. In his limited spare time, he likes to go ballroom dancing with his wife.